*Stories Based on*
the Book of Proverbs
*from the Bible*

Written by James I. Samuel
Illustrated by Carol Ruzicka

This is a work of fiction. All of the characters, names, incidents, organizations, and dialogue in this novel are either the products of the author's imagination or are used fictitiously.



WestBow Press books may be ordered through booksellers or by contacting:

WestBow Press
A Division of Thomas Nelson & Zondervan
1663 Liberty Drive
Bloomington, IN 47403
www.westbowpress.com
1 (866) 928-1240



Backcover portrait photo by RB Photography.

ISBN: 978-1-5127-9941-5 (sc)
ISBN: 978-1-5127-9940-8 (e)

Library of Congress Control Number: 2017912473

Print information available on the last page.

WestBow Press rev. date: 09/26/2017

School children from Little Roses Educational Center. Collage by Justin Mathews

# Dedication

I dedicate this book to my children, to whom I have shared most of these stories in oral form over the years.

To my parents who were an inspiration for these stories.

To my wife, Milly, who encouraged me many times to have this published.

Finally, the book is also dedicated to the children of the Little Roses Educational Center in Shiru, Kenya which is managed by InterContinental Christian Ministries (ICCM) under the guidance of Dr. O. M. Panicker. In 2015, I visited the school along with 2 friends, Alex George and Justin Mathews. The school has classes First through Eighth grade with approximately 300 children, thirteen teachers and a headmaster. Despite their circumstances, the children have a strong passion to come to the school to learn.

# Contents

# Foreword

by Ranjit Daniel

As the world becomes a global neighborhood, exposure to stories written in this book can help remind readers that the place around them contains an infinite variety of opportunities to prepare, learn, and grow. As readers, take the time to observe the characters and watch them come alive. You will relate to the characters or at least recognize familiar real-world traits in their behavior. Each provides 'pearls of wisdom' we can reflect on and incorporate into our lives.

I've known James for almost two decades and seen him grow from a freshman student at MIT to a dedicated father, talented corporate leader, caring son, cherished member of our church, and trusted friend. His gift to touch others through his calming words, friendly smile, and intelligence are exemplified in the stories written in this book. As you read these cleverly written short stories, meditate on the Proverbs the stories are based on and allow God to minister to your family through the adventures of these curious, vibrant characters.

# Preface

The Pearls of Wisdom title comes from the idiom "a pearl of wisdom", which means a voice of advice from one person to another. The Holy Bible is filled with pearls of wisdom that are beneficial for all. Some of the pearls of wisdom are allegorical, metaphorical, and even very straightforward advice. The allegorical and metaphorical pearls of wisdom are some of the best from which to create stories to enhance the meaning. Additionally, readers are more likely to remember the allegorical and metaphorical pearls of wisdom. Each of these are usually just two or three verses. Most are contained in the book of Proverbs, written by the wisest man that lived, King Solomon.

My mother always encouraged me to daily read the Bible and gave some ideas on how to do so. For example, since the book of Proverbs has 31 chapters, I should read a chapter a day for each day of a month. As a result, when I could, I would read the chapter corresponding to the day of the month. Proverbs is the book that I have probably repeatedly read since my youth.

In Proverbs, King Solomon uses simple metaphors to write about great life lessons that he has learned through experience and through his God-given intelligence. Many of these proverbs make use of animals or other natural items (like fruit). For example, Proverbs 6:6 - " Go to the ant, O sluggard, Observe her ways and be wise." With the use of animals, these proverbs are not only interesting but also timeless.

Over the years, I saw there were not many stories or books based on the Proverbs by King Solomon that could convey the meanings to young children. I wanted to convey these life lessons to children and started creating and writing these stories. With inspiration from God, I wrote these short stories and share them in this collection. Many of these stories were written over a time from 2010 onwards. I tried to use the metaphors contained in the verse to base the story and develop the lesson of the proverb. However, at times the verses prior to or after is also used to create the story.

# Introduction

The style is written like Aesop's Fables; a collection of short stories to convey a lesson or proverb. Like Aesop's Fables, some of the stories end abruptly almost like coming to the edge of a cliff and the reader must pause to ponder the meaning and lesson; or choose to continue without any consideration. However, in some cases, the stories are longer in order to really develop and arrive at the lesson. Each proverb is listed below the story.

There is no categorical ordering to the book and the short stories can be read in non-sequential order. Some of the stories also hint at other biblical stories. For example, in the "Mustard Seed" story, there are hints of Jesus' teaching on the mustard seed and the kingdom of heaven. Additionally, in some cases few of the characters are repeated. Foremost, Lady Wisdom appears in couple of stories. In the Book of Proverbs, King Solomon refers to Wisdom as Lady Wisdom. He does this to contrast wisdom with foolishness. Further, King Solomon tends to compare wisdom to a motherly figure that takes care of anyone willing to listen to her. The motherly figure provides housing, food, and advice that only a mother could provide.

All the Bible references are from the New American Standard Bible. This version is one of my favorite versions since the rhetoric is more modern while at the same time maintaining the original meaning as best as possible.

The suggestion is to read each story and the corresponding verse. Use the verse and story together to convey the meaningful lessons. The meaning and interpretation of each proverb is my own but I believe I capture the essence of the proverb and the lesson that King Solomon is trying to convey. Use this collection to teach your children. I know I will do so to teach my own children.

# Gathering Ants

One day Mr. Ant went out to gather some food. Mrs. Ant was already putting away the food Mr. Ant gathered the previous day. Mr. Ant took his children to gather the food.

As they came out of their home, they went out to the field. As they walked towards the field, a great stream stood in their way.

"What should we do Father?" asked the children.

"We'll make a bridge," replied Mr. Ant. He told them what to do and they formed a bridge out of a green leaf. They crossed over. As they continued on their path, they came to a huge rock.

"What will we do now Father?" asked the children.

"We'll have to push it children." So they pushed and pushed and together they rolled the rock away. They soon found some crumbs of bread and large pieces of nuts.

"How will we carry it all Father?"

"We'll do it little by little and we may have to come back." So they all took as much as they could and headed back.

Mr. Ant and the children walked back through the fields to where they pushed the rock and finally to their bridge. Just as they were to reach their home, Mr. Slug came out into their way.

"Where have you all been Mr. Ant?"

"We went to gather food Mr. Slug so we are ready for the winter."

"Oh Mr. Ant we still have more time before the winter comes."

"Mr. Slug you need to start gathering before the winter comes or it will be too cold." But Mr. Slug paid no attention.

Soon the cold winds of Winter blew. It was far too cold to be outside. But Mr. Ant, Mrs. Ant, and the children were safe in their home. They had enough food in the house to last all winter. A few days later, Mr. Slug knocked on Mr. Ant's door.

"Mr. Ant, I am so hungry. I tried to find food, but it is too cold and there is nothing. Will you share a little with me?"

"Oh Mr. Slug I have enough only for my family and me. Please keep looking. Did I not tell you to gather food during the summer?"

"Oh Mr. Ant I am doomed, I should have listened to you."

***Proverbs 6:6-8: Go to the ant, O sluggard, Observe her ways and be wise, which having no chief, officer or ruler, prepares her food in the summer and gathers her provision in the harvest.***

## Mustard Seed

A mustard seed met few other seeds one day. Apple, orange, lemon, pear, and many other seeds were there. To the dismay of the mustard seed, she found that of all the seeds, she was the smallest seed. The mustard seed was so upset and wished she was bigger like the other seeds. She cried and went away from the other seeds. This seed was sad that she would be little all her life and would not compare to all the other seeds. One day, the mustard seed was placed into the soil and something spectacular happened. This seed sprouted into a large tree. The small mustard seed became one of the largest trees in the garden.

***Proverbs 13:12 Hope deferred makes the heart sick, But desire fulfilled is a tree of life.***

## Bear And Rabbit

Bear and Rabbit were very good friends. They would share their meals together and would go to each other's homes, although Bear was much too large to go into Rabbit's home.

Fox did not like this friendship and wanted to split the friends. Fox went to each friend and said some words that neither Bear nor Rabbit had really said. But this greatly offended both friends. Immediately, these good friends became bitter enemies. They refused to see each other. Bear did try few times to speak to Rabbit, but Rabbit refused to even acknowledge Bear. Both even built walls around their homes just so they could not visit each other. Their hatred was so strong and even stronger than their love for each other earlier.

***Proverbs 18:19 A brother offended is harder to be won than a strong city, And contentions are like the bars of a citadel.***

## Bitter Stolen Waters

A mango tree stood between two houses. The tree was very fruitful and always had fresh sweet mangoes. But the mangoes grew on one side before the other side.

Little Donny lived on the side where the fruit came later. Mango was his favorite fruit and he longed to have one. Mother always told Donny he would have to wait for the fruit to ripen on their side of the tree. But Donny saw how the neighbor's kids always ate their ripe mangoes before he could. The light orange of the mango shined like gold in the sun. The mango looked so sweet and tasty.

Donny could no longer resist the temptation of eating the mango. He knew he would just have to wait few more days. He also knew he should not take the fruit from his neighbor's side without permission. But he set it in his heart to get the sweet mango.

One morning when Donny was to go to school and when the kids of the other house went to school, Donny hid and waited. When the time was right, Donny went to the mango tree to get a mango. On that day though, the neighbor's grandmother was looking outside. She saw someone climbing the tree and quickly called the authorities, who came to the house to find Donny sitting in the tree. He was eating the mango as though no one could see him.

Donny was caught and was told he would be held until his mom came home. He was surely in trouble. Donny started crying and now that sweet mango taste was gone from his mouth. Fortunately for Donny, the neighbor's grandmother recognized him and asked that he be set free. Donny was thankful he was free. After apologizing, Donny decided he would always wait for the mangoes on his side to ripen.

***Proverbs 9: 17-18 Stolen water is sweet; And bread eaten in secret is pleasant. But he does not know that the dead are there, That her guests are in the depths of Sheol.***

## Lady Wisdom

Wisdom, Knowledge, Understanding, Prudence, Justice were all friends. Wherever Wisdom went, the other friends were sure to follow. And wherever they went Joy soon arrived as well. They all lived together on the same street. Every morning, she would cry out very loudly and wait for someone to respond to her. As soon as she heard someone, she would rush to that person and everyone else followed. Along with these friends, Wealth and Glory also accompanied Wisdom. What a scene it was to see all these friends come to the aid of the person calling out. When Wisdom arrived, Worry, Fear, Injustice, and Sadness all ran away as quickly as they could. Wisdom would pick up the person calling, and they would dance through the streets. The person would be filled with so much wonder and happiness. The air was thick with love and gladness. All Wisdom asked was that anyone would call and listen to her instructions. Receiving Wisdom was better than getting all the gold and rubies of the world. Anyone calling out to Wisdom would surely be satisfied.

***Proverbs 8:1,11,35 Does not wisdom call, And understanding lift up her voice? For wisdom is better than jewels; And all desirable things cannot compare with her. For he who finds me finds life And obtains favor from the Lord.***

## The Farmer's Wife And The Eagle

The farmer's wife would not be satisfied with what she had on the farm. She hatched in her mind to raise a few more chickens. Although she had plenty of chickens already, she thought to raise more and more. She knew she could sell the chickens and also the eggs.

So she kept back few eggs each day. She stored it and took very good care of it. Soon the eggs hatched and few chicks came out. She fed the chicks and took very good care of them. The farmer's wife started counting the number of chickens. She started thinking of all the extra money she would get by selling the chickens and the eggs.

But one day, the eagle was watching the chicks from very high. When the farmer's wife was not looking, the eagle came sweeping down and quickly grabbed a chick. By the time the farmer's wife had turned around the eagle was very far away with the chick.

***Proverbs 23:4-5 Do not weary yourself to gain wealth, Cease from your consideration of it. When you set your eyes on it, it is gone. For wealth certainly makes itself wings like an eagle that flies toward the heavens.***

## The Ring And The Pig

Mr. Pig walked with so much pride as he prowled around the farm. Chicken, Horse, and Cow all saw the beautiful golden ring in Mr. Pig's nose. They were all surprised to see such a ring on Mr. Pig.

"How did you get that ring, Mr. Pig?" asked Chicken.

"The farmer placed it on me this very fine morning, Chicken. He surely considers me the most special animal on the farm." stated Mr. Pig.

Mr. Pig loved all the attention he was getting. But he soon grew weary of walking around showing everyone his ring. He longed to take a nice, cooling, and relaxing bath in his mud pool near his home. But he knew if he stepped into that mud bath, his golden ring would not shine as much. Each minute, he grew more and more tempted. He could no longer help himself.

He did not know whether to keep his beautiful golden ring clean or to step into his mud bath. He was becoming more and more confused and the mud bath was becoming more and more appealing. Without any hesitation, he jumped right in and muddied his beautiful golden ring. The ring did not look so beautiful anymore and the animals in the farm no longer desired to see Mr. Pig's ring ever again.

***Proverbs 11:22 As a ring of gold in a swine's snout so is a beautiful woman who lacks discretion.***

## Pleasant Words

Bear became very sick one day. So sick that he couldn't leave his den. Soon all the animal of the forest heard that Bear was sick. They all came to visit.

First the Robin came by to wish Bear well.

"Bear I've brought you some soup. You should drink that. That will make you much better!"

Bear replied, "Oh thank you good Robin. Please place it on my table. I shall take some in a little while."

Next Raccoon came by along with her two raccoon cubs.

"Bear we've brought you some very nice fruit, apples, oranges, and peaches. When you're sick, you need to eat fruit" said Raccoon.

"Thank you, " replied Bear. "Please place that on my kitchen table and I will surely eat some later."

Bear did not really want to drink any soup or eat any fruit. Bear really wanted some honey.

"Oh I wish someone would bring me a honeycomb, " thought Bear.

Just then old Owl came through the door. In his claws, he held a book.

"Bear I know Robin brought you some soup and Raccoon brought you some fruit. So I thought to bring you a book, so you can read while you rest."

"Oh Owl, you really are thoughtful. But I really want some honey. I think that would make me feel much better." replied Bear.

"Bear you can't eat any honey in your condition." replied Owl.

"But that is what I want. That is what I eat for breakfast, lunch, and dinner. Honey really is the sweetest thing in the world." replied Bear.

"Yes, you're correct Bear, " replied Owl. "But if you do not drink some soup, eat some fruit, and take some rest, you will not be able to get out of bed for many days. And it may take you a very long time for you to get some honey. Taking rest, really is the best medicine."

"I guess you are right Owl. Would you please pass me the soup and leave the book beside my bed? I will rest until I am better. I appreciate your kind words Owl," replied Bear.

Bear drank his soup, and ate some fruit. Soon he was healthy enough to run around and get some honey. Later, when Bear saw Owl, he thanked him for his wise words of wisdom.

***Proverbs 16:24 Pleasant words are a honeycomb, sweet to the soul and healing to the bones.***

## Breaching A Dam

The wise old man told the village leaders not to open the spigot from the river dam. But they did not listen. They opened it so the village would have more water. The dam was old and needed many repairs. But opening the spigot would not cause any problems, thought the leaders.

At first, everything was fine. The village received more water and the wise old man looked so foolish. But then two days later, a small crack developed on the dam. That small crack turned into a big crack. And soon enough the whole dam burst forth and the water could not be contained. The village was flooded.

***Proverbs 17:14 The beginning of strife is like letting out water, so abandon the quarrel before it breaks out.***

## The Poor Man And The Rich Man

A poor man was walking on the road back to his home. He was tired and walked very slowly. It was also not easy to walk on the rough road. After a few moments, a carriage passed by. In it was a very rich man who lived near the poor man. He could have easily given the poor man a ride, but the rich man ignored him. The poor man continued on but was so tired he decided to rest by the side of the road. While sitting there, he saw a rock that looked like an ordinary rock. But on closer inspection, the poor man realized the rock was actually a large piece of gold. This brought so much joy and happiness to the poor man. He wrapped it into his small bag and continued walking.

As the rich man went on he saw that the road was blocked by a large fallen tree. Since the road was blocked, he had to take another road, but the other road was not very clear. On this road, the tree branches hung low and the branches were getting in the eyes of the horses as well as hitting the rich man. The road was not meant for a horse drawn carriage and it became a very uncomfortable. In the meantime, the poor man walked around the fallen tree and got home. By selling the gold, the poor man lived very happily in his home.

***Proverbs 22:4-5 The reward of humility and the fear of the Lord are riches, honor and life. Thorns and snares are in the way of the perverse; He who guards himself will be far from them.***

***Proverbs 4:18 But the path of the righteous is like the light of dawn, that shines brighter and brighter until the full day.***

# The Fool And The Bear

Solomon was walking to his village through the woods. He could hear the distant grumbling of a bear. A bear that seemed very angry.

Solomon kept walking and soon came to a clearing. To his astonishment, there stood the bear. A female bear who seemed ready to attack. Turning around, Solomon could also see a wolf with a bear cub in the wolf's mouth. The mother bear was ready to charge. Solomon ran quickly back to his village.

The roar of the bear was still loud in his ears and soon he heard the howling of an injured wolf. Solomon knew he was safe and went to his village to warn his people of the angry bear.

As he entered the village, to his utter shock, there stood the Village Fool holding a bear cub. The bear had not lost one cub, but in fact 2 cubs.

"What have you done fool? You have brought destruction to us all. Soon the mother bear will be in the village and soon that bear would attack the whole village."

***Proverbs 17:12 Let a man meet a bear robbed of her cubs, rather than a fool in his folly.***

## Diligence

A wicked king had a great deal of land but was always greedy to have more. He always was deceptive in how he fooled the owners of the land. Many times, he bought the land at a much lower price than the actual value. He did this by befriending the owner and showing much love to the owner. In the end the owner was willing to sell his land at a much smaller price.

One day this king saw the land of Lord Diligence. Lord Diligence was a man that was not easily fooled. So the king invited Lord Diligence to his palace. To be invited to the palace was a great honor in the land.

When Lord Diligence arrived, there was set before him a table with all the delicate foods. The food looked so delicious. But Lord Diligence knew the tricks of this king. He controlled what he ate and did not let the king fool him. The king saw that Lord Diligence did not indulge himself and realized he could not use the same tricks he used to fool the other land owners. Lord Diligence was fortunate to not fall in to the traps of this wicked king.

***Proverbs 23:1-3 When you sit down to dine with a ruler, consider carefully [a]what is before you, and put a knife to your throat if you are a man of great appetite. Do not desire his delicacies, for it is deceptive food.***

## The Woodpecker

A woodpecker loved to peck in his forest home. All his other woodpecker friends and family were also there. But this woodpecker would fly far away from his own tree and peck on the very outside of his forest. He thought the juicy bugs and worms were tastier on the outside of the forest. His family and friends warned him not to go to the outside of the forest. On the outside of the forest, the hunters could use their rifles to shoot the bird down. But the woodpecker did not listen to their words. One day as the woodpecker pecked on the outskirts of the forest a hunter spotted him. The sharp marksman aimed and forever stopped this woodpecker's pecking.

***Proverbs 27:8 Like a bird that wanders from her nest, so is a man who wanders from his home.***

***Proverbs 5:15 Drink water from your own cistern and fresh water from your own well.***

## Neither Right Nor Left

A child was lost in the woods
Of only seven years old was she
Which way to turn, she did not know
She sat down to cry,
But instead looked up to the sky

There in the night was a star
As bright as a jewel
Do not cry child, just follow me
And I'll lead you home but only
Look neither right nor left

So the child stood and followed
She wanted to look right or left
But kept her gaze on the bright star
She stayed directly on the straight path
And followed the star out from the woods

Soon she saw her home
There was her mother looking for the child
Mother and child hugged very long
She had reached her home following the star
By looking neither right nor left

***Proverbs 4:25, 27 Let your eyes look directly ahead and let your [a]gaze be fixed straight in front of you. Do not turn to the right nor to the left; turn your foot from evil.***

## Lady Wisdom's Home

Lady Wisdom has a beautiful home. The home has 7 pillars and is open to many visitors. In fact, Lady Wisdom goes out and invites anyone to visit her. She lets anyone know that by visiting her home, those visitors will have more understanding and knowledge. This is a promise she makes to all that will visit her. She has prepared delicious meals that once you enter her home, you will not want to leave. She also promises that by accepting her, all her visitors will have a longer life and better understanding.

***Proverbs 9:1-6 Wisdom has built her house, she has hewn out her seven pillars; She has prepared her food, she has mixed her wine; She has also set her table; She has sent out her maidens, she calls from the tops of the heights of the city: "Whoever is naive, let him turn in here!" To him who lacks understanding she says, "Come, eat of my food and drink of the wine I have mixed. "Forsake your folly and live, and proceed in the way of understanding."***

## The Bold Lion

All the animals of the forest started to run. Raccoon asked to Fox "What's wrong? Why are we all running?"

Fox replied, "Actually I'm not sure why we are running, but you know how we animals are. If everyone is running, there must be a reason. So, keep running!"

Soon they all ran past Lion who was not running but looking sternly beyond the rushing animals. Lion started to smile. He immediately realized what had spooked all the animals. A strong wind had rustled and shaken the trees. The animals thought hunters were coming into the forest and chasing them. Lion stood boldly and roared loudly.

***Proverbs 28:1 The wicked flee when no one is pursuing, But the righteous are bold as a lion.***

## Horses In Battle

All the horses were readied for the battle. Each horse had a full body armor. The saddles for the horse were made of iron. On the horses' head was placed armor that covered almost everything except for the horse's eyes and mouth. The soldier, with full armor, mounted the horse.

He rode the horse out to the top of the hill. Many of the soldiers knew this battle would be different and tensions were very high. However, as all the mounted soldiers reached the top of the hill overlooking the valley, they noticed the enemy was nowhere to be seen. Something had scared off the enemy and they had fled from their camp. The battle was over and won before it ever began.

***Proverbs 21:31 The horse is prepared for the day of battle, But victory belongs to the Lord.***

## Free Yourself

Bird was so worried. He had borrowed some food from Squirrel. Now he did not know how to pay Squirrel back. Bird was getting very depressed thinking about all of this and was not paying attention to where he was going. Suddenly, he was caught in a trap. A bird hunter caught him and put him into cage. Bird thought there was no hope to escape from this cage. While the hunter was not looking, Bird tried with all his might to get himself free. Finally, he saw that the opening of the cage was starting loosen up. The hunter was still not paying attention. Bird tried few more times and with that the cage door opened. He flew out immediately and as fast he could. The hunter could not respond quick enough to catch him again.

*Proverbs 6:1-5 My son, if you have become surety for your neighbor, have given a pledge for a stranger, if you have been snared with the words of your mouth, have been caught with the words of your mouth, do this then, my son, and deliver yourself; Since you have come into the hand of your neighbor, Go, humble yourself, and importune your neighbor. Give no sleep to your eyes, nor slumber to your eyelids; deliver yourself like a gazelle from the hunter's hand and like a bird from the hand of the fowler.*

CPSIA information can be obtained
at www.ICGtesting.com
Printed in the USA
BVOW10s0516081217
501900BV00014B/87/P